P9-DTB-318

MATT MYERS

Hum and Swish

NEAL PORTER BOOKS

HOLIDAY HOUSE / NEW YORK

Neal Porter Books

Text and illustrations copyright © 2019 by Matt Myers
All Rights Reserved
HOLIDAY HOUSE is registered in the U.S. Patent and Trademark Office.
Printed and bound in November 2018 at Toppan Leefung, DongGuan City, China.
The artwork for this book was created with acrylic and oil paint.
Book design by Jennifer Browne
www.holidayhouse.com
First Edition
1   3   5   7   9   10   8   6   4   2

Library of Congress Cataloging-in-Publication Data

Names: Myers, Matt, author, illustrator.
Title: Hum and swish / Matt Myers.
Description: First edition. | New York : Holiday House, [2019] | "Neal Porter
Books." | Summary: Jamie wants to quietly work on an art project near her
friend, the sea, but people keep disturbing her by asking questions.
Identifiers: LCCN 2018030128 | ISBN 9780823442867 (hardcover)
Subjects: | CYAC: Art—Fiction. | Questions and answers—Fiction. |
Beaches—Fiction.
Classification: LCC PZ7.M99123 Hum 2019 | DDC [E]—dc23 LC record available
at https://lccn.loc.gov/2018030128

For Maya,
the first person I want to show my creations to

Jamie and the sea are friends.

Jamie hums. The waves swish.

People come and go, asking questions.

"What are you making there?"

"I don't know," Jamie says.

"I don't know," Jamie says.

"Isn't that pretty?"

"I don't know," Jamie says.

"What's that supposed to be?"

"I don't know," Jamie says.

"How cute is that?"

The waves swish.

Jamie hums.

The sea tells stories, but it doesn't ask questions.

Jamie's dad brings sunblock. "Is that a horse?"

"Maybe," Jamie says.

Jamie's mom brings a juice box. "When do you think you might be finished with your project?"

"Not sure," Jamie says.

Hum. Swish.

Someone else comes.

She brings a lot of things,

but no questions.

"What are you making?" Jamie asks.

"I don't know yet."

"Me neither," Jamie says.

Jamie and the sea and the woman are friends.

Jamie hums.

The woman swishes
her paintbrush in a jar.

"I think I'm done,"
Jamie says.

"Me too."